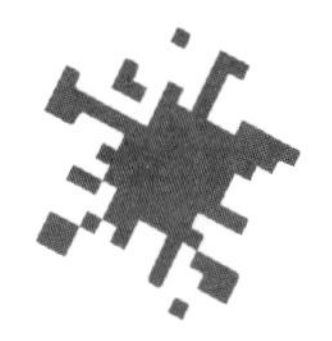

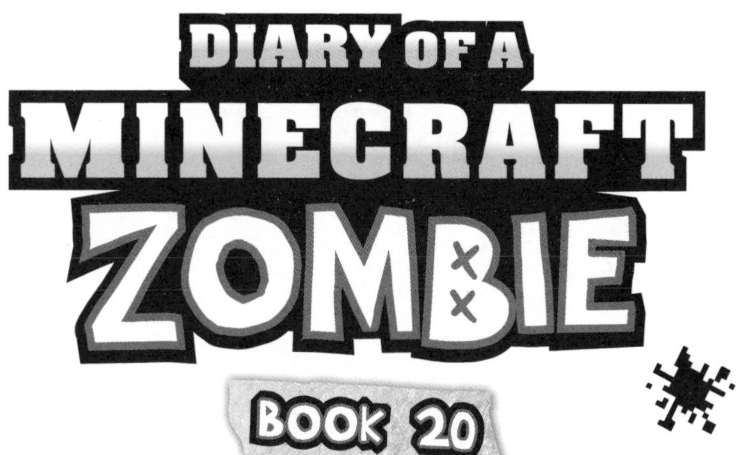

MOB MASH

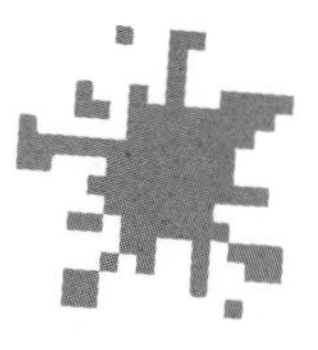

Koala Books
An imprint of Scholastic Australia Pty Limited
PO Box 579 Gosford NSW 2250
ABN 11 000 614 577
www.scholastic.com.au

Part of the Scholastic Group
Sydney • Auckland • New York • Toronto • London • Mexico City
New Delhi • Hong Kong • Buenos Aires • Puerto Rico

Published by Scholastic Australia in 2019.

A catalogue record for this book is available from the National Library of Australia

ISBN 978-1-76066-561-6

Typeset in Agent 'C', AgencyFB, Potato Cut TT and Bender.

Printed in China by Hang Tai Printing Company Limited.

Scholastic Australia's policy, in association with Hang Tai Printing Company, is to use papers that are renewable and made efficiently from wood grown in responsibly managed forests, so as to minimise its environmental footprint.

23 24 25 / 2

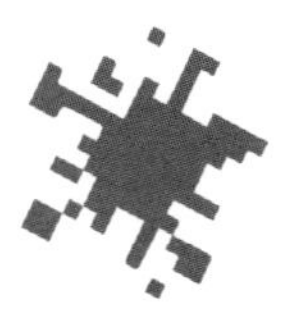

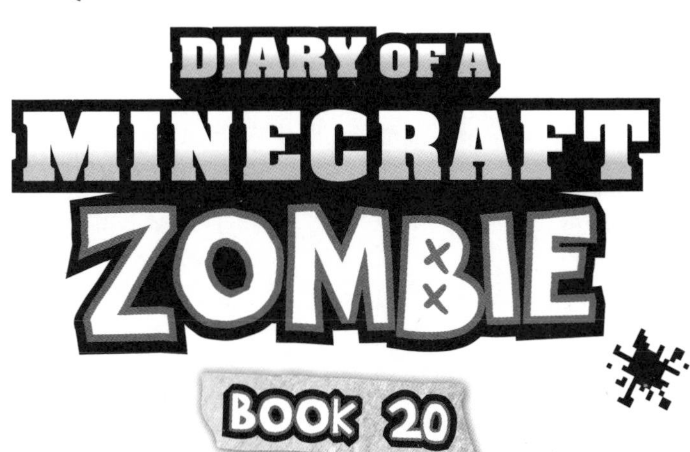

Mob Mash

BY

Zack Zombie

Koala Books

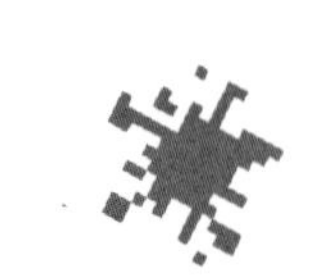

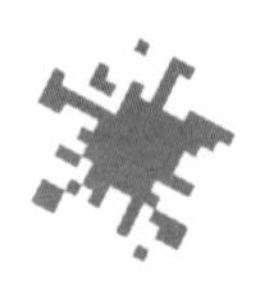

TUESDAY

PLONK!

Mum set my breakfast down in front of me, then sat at the table and **STARED** at me.

Uh… okay.

I didn't know what else to do, so I started eating.

'Zombie,' Mum said with a sigh.

'Mmmfffmmmm,' I nodded, my mouth full.

She paused, then sighed again.

'Zombie, I have a friend coming to visit from my hometown. Do you remember how the Aliens came and pretty much **DESTROYED** it?'

I nodded again, my mouth now full of orange juice.

'Well, my friend Eloise is moving biomes because her home was ruined. They will be staying with us for a couple of days.'

I just continued to nod.

'Eloise will be here with her daughter. Zombie... please don't be **WEIRD** around her. Endaria is a sweet girl, and you can be really... odd sometimes.'

'GGHGH-HEY!' I spluttered food all over the table in indignation.

'Just be nice,' Mum said. 'They are arriving today, so they will be here when you get home from school, and they'll leave on Saturday.'

I met Creepy, Slimey and Skelee at lunchtime.

'And get this,' I said, shovelling food into my mouth, 'Mum said, "don't be weird". As if I'm weird all the time.'

The guys all **CRACKED UP.**

'Yeah!' I laughed too. 'Crazy, right?! Calling me weird, pffft!' I scoffed.

Creepy gasped for air and tried to stop laughing. 'No, Zombie, we're not laughing with you. We're laughing *at* you. You definitely need warning. You're *so* weird!' He burst out laughing again.

'What?! How am I weird?!'

But the guys couldn't stop laughing before the bell rang and lunch finished. I never found out why they think I'm weird.

'MUM, I'M HOME!' I almost kicked the front door in with enthusiasm. It was the end of the school day, which meant **AFTER-SCHOOL SNACKS!** My second favourite snack category.

My first favourite snack category is post-adventure snacks. There's nothing quite like destroying a villain, saving the Overworld and then having a snack.

Preferably cake.

'MUUUUUUUUUM!' I yelled again.

'Zombie!' Mum called out from the living room. 'I'm in here.'

I dropped my backpack at the foot of the stairs and stomped towards the kitchen. 'I'm in a **CAKEY MOOD**, Mum. Do we have any?'

I stepped into the living room and realised my mum wasn't alone.

That's when I locked eyes with **THE MOST BEAUTIFUL GIRL** I had ever seen.

The air whooshed out of my chest. It felt like time went into slow motion. Everything started to go hazy and I couldn't focus.

Then I fainted.

WEDNESDAY

'Okay, so I think I get where my mum was coming from when she said "don't be weird",' I said to Slimey on the way to school.

'Oh no. What did you do, Zombie?' If Slimey had arms, I think he would have **FACE-PALMED.**

'I fainted.'

'You what?' Slimey obviously wasn't expecting that answer.

'I laid eyes on her: Endaria, the most beautiful mob in all the galaxies—'

'We're in the Overworld, we don't have galaxies,' Slimey interrupted.

'Whatever. Trust me, you've never seen anyone like her. I'm in **LOVE.**'

'Uh... okay. But have you spoken to her?'

'Slimey, speaking is secondary. I'm in love. You wouldn't understand. Plus I was passed out all night. Missed dinner and everything. But don't worry, I have a plan!'

'Plan? For what?' Creepy interrupted.

By that point we had gotten to school and the rest of the crew had joined us. I explained that I was in love and had to impress Endaria.

'Okay, hit me. What's the plan?' Creepy said excitedly.

'I'm gonna practise some **PICK-UP LINES** and wow her with them!'

The guys didn't look impressed.

'Are you a pimple? Cause I want you on my arm,' I said with a cheeky grin.

'Eww.'

'Zombie, that's gross.'

Clearly the guys **WEREN'T IMPRESSED.** 'Okay, well, maybe that one's a Zombie one.'

'Is she a Zombie?' Creepy asked.

'Uh no, she's an Enderman.'

'Okay, then try some Enderman ones,' Skelee said helpfully.

'Hmm, right. That makes sense. Hey, girl, I'm pretty handy, so I must be what you've been missing all your life.'

Skelee slowly nodded. 'Ok...ay.'

'**GET IT?**' I said. 'Cause Endermen don't have hands. So she needs hands. And I'm handy...'

'That's probably a bit rude...' Creepy said doubtfully.

'Okay, fine. I'm all out.' I sat down with a plop. 'What am I gonna do?!'

Just then Heather Huskly walked by and waved at us. 'Hey, guys. See you in class!'

'Hey, Heather,' we all called back.

'Dude, that's it! I have the best idea!' Slimey said excitedly. **'HAVE A PARTY!'**

'What?' I was confused.

'Heather Huskly had a party and she is one of the coolest girls in school now. That will impress Endaria. Everyone loves a party.'

'Yeah, but Heather was already cool when she threw the party,' Creepy said.

'And what, I'm not?' I said defensively.

The guys all looked at each other and started shuffling their feet.

'Hey, I'm **TOTALLY COOL!**' I exclaimed. 'Okay, let's do this! We'll invite a bunch of classmates and make it really cool and Endaria will fall in love with me. It'll be the greatest party ever!' I said excitedly.

'Yeah!' the guys cheered.

'I guess the only thing you need to figure out now is how to throw a good party,' Skelee said.

Oh yeah. **THAT.**

THURSDAY

'Okay,' I said. The guys were sitting in a row on my bed after school and I was marching back and forth in front of them like a **DRILL SERGEANT.**

'Our mission is to throw the

GREATEST PARTY EVER.

First off, no party is a cool party unless there are no parents. We have to get my parents and Endaria's mum out of the house. Any ideas, team?'

I turned to the guys. You could have heard a block drop in the silence.

'Come on, guys! No ideas? What are you even doing here then?' I said in frustration.

'To be honest, I don't know what I'm doing here.'

'AAAAAAAGGHHHHH!' I shrieked and almost fell over.

I looked behind me, and sitting quietly on my deskchair was Ellie, Creepy's cousin.

'How long have you been there?' I asked, panting for breath.

'The better question is how long have you known you could hit such a **HIGH NOTE,**' Ellie laughed. 'Man, that was impressive! But if you're trying to impress this Endaria girl, try not to scream in front of her. You sound like a Pig whose candy corn was stolen!'

'That's not helpful,' I said. Mentally, I made a note to avoid getting scared in front of Endaria.

'What are you doing here anyway?' I asked.

'Creepy and I were supposed to go home together after school, but he was coming here so I tagged along,' Ellie said with a grin. 'So, what's the go? What's crackin'? What **SNEAKY** adventures are we up to now?'

'Nothing sneaky,' I said defensively. 'The thing is, I'm in love. So I'm gonna throw a party to get Endaria to like me.'

Ellie nodded. 'Okay... that seems well thought out.'

'Thanks!' I said. 'Anyway, I need my parents **OUT OF THE HOUSE** on Friday after school.'

'Zombie!' My mum knocked on the door and entered. 'Oh hello! I didn't know you had friends over, Zombie! Do you guys want any snacks? Cookies? Licorice sticks?'

'Oh yes, please!'

'That would be great, Mrs Z.'

'Thanks so much, ma'am!'

You'd think they were all here for a good time, not an important **MISSION PLANNING SESSION.**

'Mum, did you need something?' I interrupted.

'Oh yes. Just letting you know that Eloise, your father and I are going to watch a movie tomorrow after you get home from school.

I've organised a babysitter for Wesley—' I started to interupt but she put up her hand to stop me and kept talking. 'I know that you've insisted you're old enough, so the babysitter isn't for you. Endaria doesn't want to come to the movie so you can entertain her. Play board games or something, okay?'

My mum smiled at everyone, then left the room.

'Oh wow, did that just fall into your lap like a well-timed drop **OR WHAT?!**' Creepy said excitedly.

'Yes!' I cheered. 'Part one of the

MISSION ACCOMPLISHED.

I just have to keep Wesley's babysitter out of the way.'

FRIDAY

'Hey, party at my place after school today. **COOL KIDS ONLY,**' I grinned and handed out party flyers to the mob kids in my class.

Then I went and sat down next to Creepy. 'This is gonna be the best party ever.'

'Man, I am so excited. Are you gonna have games? Snacks? A disco ball?'

'Uhhh, I hadn't thought about it,' I said.

'What?!' Creepy did not look happy. 'Your party is tonight and you've literally planned **NOTHING?**'

I shrugged.

'Well, lucky for you I am an expert in this kinda stuff. First things first—we need a disco ball. Don't worry, I know a guy.'

'Don't say anything,' Creepy hissed at me as we walked through the playground. Well, I walked, Creepy hopped.

'Why?' I asked.

'Just don't.' Creepy hopped towards the **BIGGEST** Skeleton I had ever seen. He was at least four times the size of Skelee.

'Hey there, Skeletor!' Creepy called. The Skeleton was so big that Creepy and I had to crane our heads back to make anything close to eye contact. He was like the Skeleton version of my giant Zombie friend, Mutant. 'What's been happening?'

'They're making me repeat third grade again,' Skeletor said really slowly. He sounded like someone had taken a regular voice and **SLOWED** it right down.

'Oh man, that sucks,' Creepy said. 'Maybe you'll get it this time?

Eighth time's the charm, right?'

Skeletor just nodded slowly.

'Anyway, this is my friend, Zombie. He needs a **DISCO BALL.**'

'Hey, Zombie,' Skeletor waved at me slowly. Everything he did was in slow motion. 'What do you need a disco ball for?'

'I'm having a party, cool kids only. Gotta make sure it's the best party ever!' I grinned and gave Skeletor a thumbs up. Then I turned and winked at Creepy.

He looked like he wanted to stuff a sock in my mouth.

'Party?' Skeletor said slowly.

'Oh, pfft, it's nothing,' Creepy said.

'I love parties.'

'Oh.'

We stood in **AWKWARD SILENCE.** Creepy shot daggers at me with his eyes and then turned back to Skeletor.

'Hey, Skeletor, you wanna come to the party? It's tonight.'

Creepy forced a smile.

'Oh yeah, that sounds fun!' Skeletor clapped his hands... **SLOWLY.**

THUD.

THUD.

THUD.

'And about that disco ball...?' Creepy asked hopefully.

'Oh, I have one lying around somewhere. I'll bring it when we swing by later tonight.'

'W-w-we?' I stammered.

'Oh, just me and the boys. See you guys later!' He turned and trudged away.

'What did I say?' Creepy hissed.

'Umm...'

'Don't speak! And guess what you did?!'

'... Speak?'

Creepy looked like he wanted to push me into a pit of **LAVA.**

'It's not my fault I forgot—I have a **PEA-SIZED BRAIN!'** I said.

Creepy sighed. 'You better hope we have enough snacks for Skeletor and his buddies now.'

FRIDAY 6:00

'Okay, BYE MUM!' I tried to usher her out the door. The guests weren't arriving for another hour, but the guys were going to be over any minute to help me set up.

I'd told Creepy to bring music and Slimey and Skelee to bring snacks and decorations. I'd also invited Steve, but I gave him strict instructions—be

UNNOTICEABLE.

RING, RING! RING, RING!

'Oh hang on, one second,' Mum fished her zPhone out of her bag and answered it. 'Hi! Are you on your way? Oh. Hmm. Oh dear, that's no good, is it? Oh no. Oh, you poor thing. It's coming from where? **PROJECTILE?!** Don't worry. Alright, you take care now. Bye!'

Mum hung up the phone and looked at Eloise, 'I am so sorry, Eloise, I think we're going to have to cancel. My babysitter just called in sick, so there is no one to look after Wesley.'

What...

What!

WHAT IS HAPPENING?!

NO-NO-NO-NO-NO-NO-NO—

NOT ON MY WATCH!

'Oh no, Mum, that's terrible! I bet you really wanted to see that movie...' I put on my best "**SAD SON**" look.

'It was going to be lovely. A historically accurate depiction of the pre-gaming era—'

'Yeah, that sounds great, but I have an idea,' I interrupted. 'What if I watched Wesley?'

Mum scowled at me. 'The first time we left you alone with him, you lost him in a sewer, the second time, you blew up the house, the third time, the house burned down, the fourth time, you—'

'Yeah, but that's all in the past!' I said hastily. 'I've **GROWN UP** since then. I can look after a measly little Chicken Jockey!'

Mum didn't look convinced.

'Plus,' I waved in the general direction of the hallway behind me, 'Endaria is here! Have you ever met someone more **RESPONSIBLE?'**

'That is very true.' Mum looked at Eloise.

'Endaria did used to babysit for our old neighbours,' Eloise offered.

'Yeah, I love Wesley!' Endaria said. 'He and I get along great. Plus, you guys deserve a night out. You work so hard taking care of us and don't get enough time to yourself. It'll be a breeze. Right now, it's my track record against Zombie's!' Endaria laughed at her own joke and I almost fainted again. It sounded like **WIND CHIMES** and I loved it so much it made me want to throw up.

'Okay, fine. But make sure you guys look after Wesley and put him to bed by 7:00.' Mum looked at me sternly. 'And Zombie... do not touch anything flammable. At all.'

'Okay, okay!' I was too scared to say anything else in case she changed her mind.

My dad hadn't said a word the whole time. Now he **WINKED** at me and followed Mum and Eloise out the door.

As soon as they were gone, I turned to Endaria. 'I hope you don't mind, but I have a couple of friends coming over.'

'Sure, no worries. It's your house,' she smiled and walked back down the hall.

'You know, cause I'm really cool. People wanna come and hang out with me all the time. A lot of people!' I called after her.

'Okay, Zombie! Whatever you say,' she said over her shoulder as she climbed the stairs.

Well, that worked out well.

Part two of the **MISSION ACCOMPLISHED!**

FRIDAY 6:11

DING, DONG!

I ran to the door and threw it open. Slimey, Skelee and Creepy were standing on the doorstep, carrying bags of supplies.

'Alright, guys, mission is a go. Parents are gone, but there is a **PROBLEM.** The babysitter bailed and we're stuck with Wesley.'

'Oh man,' Creepy huffed.

'It's okay, I have a plan!' I said excitedly. 'He's already had an early dinner, so I'll just put him to bed and shut him in his room. That way he won't be around to **EMBARRASS** us.'

Slimey looked unsure, but I ignored that and marched ahead with the plan. 'Alright, it's happening. Let's get set up.'

Endaria was playing with Wesley in his room, which gave us the perfect cover to start putting decorations up.

Skelee pointed at different bags as he said, 'Okay, we have balloons, streamers, food and drinks.'

'Excellent.' I rubbed my hands together in excitement and started rummaging through the bags. Then I stopped, pulled a tangled mess of streamers out of the bag and looked at Skelee in **HORROR.**

'WHY IS IT ALL PINK?'

'What?' Skelee was confused. 'Is that bad?'

'Skelee!' I yelled. 'This isn't a

baby's party! It's a disaster!'

'I dunno, man! Why did you tell me to organise decorations? I don't have **EYEBALLS!**' Skelee said defensively.

I poked through the bags. Everything was pink. The streamers, the balloons...

What was I going to do now?

'Oh man, that's so cool!'

I whirled around and Endaria was walking towards us. She held up a pink streamer and beamed at me.

'I **LOVE** the colour pink. All this stuff looks great.'

'YES! YES, IT DOES!' I shouted.

'Ow,' Endaria put her arms over her ears. 'Why are you shouting?'

I lowered my voice. 'Haha, I don't know, sorry. Hahahahahahahaha. But I love pink too. Hahaha. Doesn't it look great? We're gonna set the place up.'

'Sure,' Endaria smiled and walked off.

'Dude...' Creepy said. 'I'm confused. 'You just called this a disaster and yelled at Skelee. Now it's perfect?'

I snapped my fingers in front of him, accidentally breaking one off. 'Get with the program, Creepy,' I said as I twisted my finger back on. 'Endaria said she likes pink, so now everything will be pink. **EVERYTHING!** BRB, guys. I gotta go get changed.'

Twenty minutes later I returned in the same clothes.

'What—'

'Don't ask,' I shrugged. 'Turns out I don't actually *have* any pink clothes. Only turquoise and blue.' I looked at my outfit sadly. 'Endaria will **NEVER** love me.'

'Okay, but while *you've* been mucking around, we've set everything up! Look!' Slimey showed off the living room excitedly.

The streamers had been hung up, balloons littered the floor, the food and drinks were out, and the cups were neatly stacked with a marker nearby so people could write their names.

'Dudes...' I said in shock. 'This actually looks **AWESOME!** You guys did such a good job!'

'Thanks!' Slimey grinned.

I went over to the speakers and put one of Creepy's music discs on. *Zombie Walk* by Dead-ication started playing and I turned up the volume and bopped my head.

'**NOW** we're ready. Bring on the party!'

FRIDAY 7:14

We'd been nibbling on snacks for about ten minutes before the doorbell rang. I raced to the door and smoothly pulled it open. 'Welcome to my...'

I trailed off when I saw Skeletor standing there. The problem was, he wasn't standing there alone. He had four other Skeletons with him. And they were all the same size as him... that is, **HUGE.**

'Hi,' I said meekly.

'Hello,' Skeletor waved slowly. He thrust a bag at me and then marched inside with his friends.

Endaria poked her head out of Wesley's room upstairs. 'I put Wesley to bed. Hey, whatcha got there?'

'Oh hey!' I grinned at her.

She came down and looked at the bag Skeletor had handed me. I opened it.

It was a giant **DISCO BALL.**

'Wow!' Endaria looked impressed.

'Looks like it'll be a good party. I hope you guys have a fun time.' She smiled sadly and started to head back upstairs.

Hang on... isn't she coming to the party? She has to or my whole plan will have been for nothing!

Wait... did I ever actually invite her?!

URGH!

'Hey, Endaria,' I called out. 'You don't have to hang out in Wesley's room all night.'

'Really?' She turned back to me in surprise.

'Yeah!' I nodded. 'I thought, you know, you could, like, come hang out with us!'

'Oh,' she smiled. 'I thought I was Wesley's **BABYSITTER** for the night.'

'Pfft, no! I just said that so I could get our parents out of the house!' I explained.

'Oh. Well, then I'd love to hang out with you guys.' Endaria smiled and followed me into the living room.

I stopped. I'd forgotten about Skeletor. He was talking, slowly, to Creepy. Creepy looked like he wanted to **EXPLODE** on purpose and take everyone out with him. I sighed—better go rescue him.

I introduced Endaria to everyone, including Skeletor and his mates, trying to be casual.

Then I pulled a chair over to the middle of the living room and sticky-taped the disco ball to the ceiling.

'Perfect!'

After a few more laps around the room, trying to look cool and casual, I pulled Creepy aside.

'Creepy, is everyone having **FUN?**'

'Uhh... I think so?'

'What do you mean, you "think so"? They HAVE to be having fun. Especially Endaria. How do I make the party more fun?' I was starting to stress.

'Woah... chill, dude.'

DING, DONG!

'Yes! More people. That'll make this more fun!' I opened the door and saw half my class there. 'Hey, guys! Welcome!' I held the door wide open for everyone. I was nailing this whole '**HOSTING**' thing!

By the time I made it back to the living room, everyone was talking to each other...

Wait, who was *that*?!

There was a Creeper I didn't know talking to Endaria, and, horror, she was **LAUGHING** at his jokes.

Oh no, what if she was starting to like him?

FRIDAY 7:47

'Hey there,' I said, as I broke in on Endaria and the mysterious Creeper she was talking to.

'Hey-o, buddy-o!' the Creeper nodded happily at me. 'I heard this is your house-io. Great PARTY-O. Loving the snacks-io.'

I shot a look at Endaria and she just shrugged.

'I'm Zombie.' I waved at the weird Creeper.

'I'm Ste... Creep...io,' the Creeper said.

Huh?

'Do you go to school with us?' I asked.

'Oh yes, school-io! You must remember seeing me around-io!' Ste-Creepio laughed.

'Alright...' I wasn't convinced.

'Hey-o, Zombie-o, could you show me where the **MOULDSHAKES** are? I want a top up-io!' The strange Creeper shoulder-bumped me cheerfully.

'Sure.' I was glad to lead Ste-Creepio away from Endaria.

As we were walking towards the drinks table, the Creeper pushed me into the hallway.

'Hey! Watch it, man!'

'Dude!' The Creeper pulled off a **MASK.**

'STEVE?!'

'SHHH!' Steve covered my mouth and pushed me into the empty kitchen. 'How do you like my disguise?' He grinned and spun in a circle.

'You're dressed as a Creeper?' I asked.

'Well, yeah!' Steve made a **TA-DA** motion with his hands. 'What did you expect me to do? Walk in here dressed as a Human?'

I shrugged. 'Why are you talking weird though? Creepers don't talk like that.'

'I wanted to throw the scent off my disguise,' Steve explained. 'If anyone starts to think my disguise looks weird, they'll be so confused by how I talk, they'll forget about the costume!'

'Actually, that's **GENIUS.**'

'Why, thank you!' Steve tried to bow, but his costume got stuck halfway. 'Anyway, why were you all weird back there?'

'Cause you were talking to Endaria! She's the whole reason I'm throwing this party, dude.' I sighed. 'I'm in love and I want her to notice me.'

Steve looked confused. 'I think she's already noticed you, man. She's staying in your house.'

'Yeah, but now I need her to **LIKE** me.'

'And this party is going to do that... how?'

I sighed again. 'This is gonna be the best party ever. Everyone is gonna have an amazing time, including Endaria. I will become crazy popular at school, Endaria will realise everyone else loves me and she will fall in love with me too.'

Steve snorted. 'I don't think—'

'I don't want to hear it!' I held a hand up to stop him talking. 'My plan is **PERFECT.**'

'Okay.' Steve peeked across the hall into the living room, then turned back to me. 'Well, you can't keep intercepting the mobs around Endaria all night.'

'What's "intercepting"?'

'Like... cutting in when someone is talking to her.'

'Well, then yes, I can. That is exactly my plan and I'm gonna do it all night. I can't have her fall in love with someone else before she has the chance to fall in love with me!'

'Yeah, well, **GOOD LUCK,** cause a bunch of giant Skeletons are talking to her now!'

I peeked around Steve. It was a

lot more **CROWDED** than I remembered. Who were all these mobs? I must be cooler than I thought. I finally spotted Endaria chatting to Skeletor and his buddies.

'NOOOOO!' I wailed. 'Steve, what do I do?' I grabbed Steve by the shoulders of his Creeper costume and shook him.

'Alright, hang on.' Steve fixed his costume, which had fallen sideways with the shaking. 'Don't intercept Endaria all night. Let her talk to other people. Don't be the weird, jealous guy. Just be **YOURSELF.** She'll see how cool and awesome you are.'

'But Steve! I'M NOT COOL! IT'S ALL A LIE. I'M NOT AWESOME AT ALL!' I wailed again.

'Dude, you are! And even if you don't feel like it, just "fake it till you make it"!' Steve bopped his head against mine.

I nodded. 'Okay, I can do this. I'll just go out there and be cool. "Fake it till you make it".'

'Man, being a Creeper is really hard,' Steve said. 'How do they cope without **HANDS?!**'

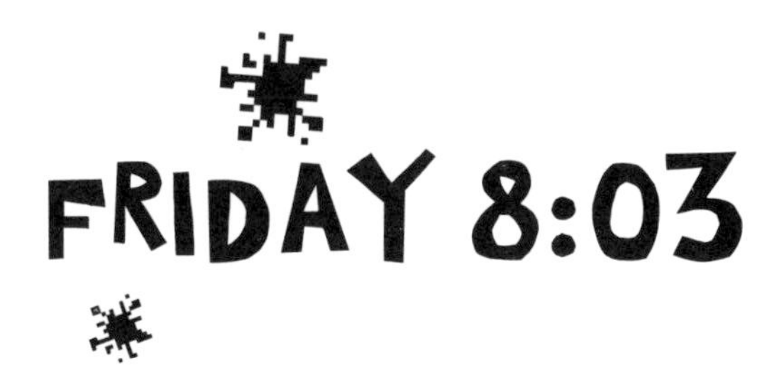

FRIDAY 8:03

When I snuck back into the living room after talking to Steve, I had to push through the crowd to find Skelee.

'It's a lot more crowded than I remember...'

'Yeah, we just left the door open cause we got **SICK** of answering the doorbell,' Skelee explained.

'I don't remember handing out this many flyers.'

'Zombie, focus. We've got bigger problems.'

'What?'

'I think we're gonna run out of food,' Skelee waved at the snacks table, which looked like it had been **ATTACKED** by a pack of rabid Ocelots.

'Is that bad?' I asked.

'Yeah, it's bad! What are the mobs gonna eat? What if they decide to leave cause they get hungry?'

'Hey, Zombie! Great party!' Heather

Huskly waved as she walked by. 'Pity about the **SNACKS** though... I'm a bit hungry!'

'We can go back to my house if you're still hungry? My mum usually has cake,' Heather's friend, Betty Blaze, offered.

'NO!' I shouted. 'Don't do that. I've got more food! I just forgot to put it out. Hahahaha...'

Heather and Betty just smiled and edged away.

'Yeah. Okay. Tip for you, buddy,' Skelee said, 'don't laugh like that again. It's creepy. And not the Creeper Creepy we know.'

I dragged Skelee to the kitchen and forced him to rummage through the cupboards with me.

'Umm... I found some mushrooms. We could make **MUSHROOM STEW?'**

'Ew, dude. Who wants to eat mushroom stew at a party?! Keep looking.' I pulled out a pumpkin and sugar.

'I found an egg!' Skelee waved the egg at me from near the fridge.

'Yes!' I dragged the egg, sugar and pumpkin to the crafting table and threw it all together.

BAM!

Pumpkin pie!

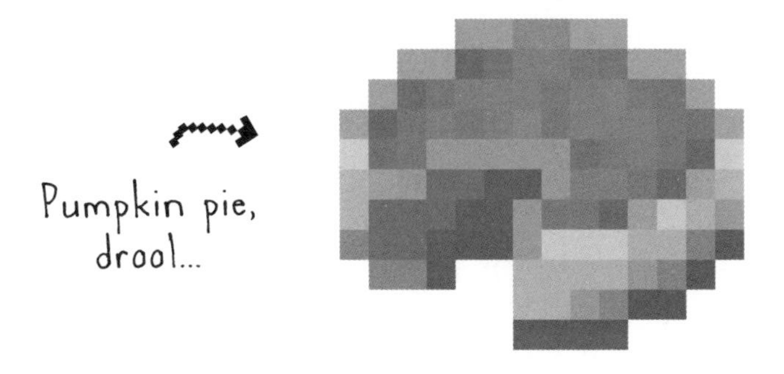

'Yes!' Skelee and I high-fived each other. 'What else?'

'I found Cocoa Pods,' Skelee offered.

'Oh wait, dude! I found some wheat earlier!' I shuffled through the cupboards again before I found the wheat. 'Yes! You know what this means?'

'Uh... we have wheat?' Skelee shrugged.

'We can make **COOKIES!**' I arranged the wheat and Cocoa Pods on the crafting table. 'Come on, man, get with the program.'

'Dude, I don't eat,' Skelee shrugged.

BAM!

'And now we have cookies! Do you reckon that will be enough?' I asked Skelee.

'Oh, hang on! I know someone who has a beetroot crop!' Skelee said excitedly. 'Let me get some **BEETROOT!'**

'Uhh, okay,' I said slowly. I didn't know what we were going to make with beetroot, but Skelee seemed excited, so I let it go.

'WAIT HERE!' Skelee bolted out of the room like a Skeleton dodging sunlight.

I had only been waiting a couple minutes, when—

CRASHHHH!

I ran into the living room and saw a chunk of blocks missing from the ceiling. Oh man, there would be no fixing that before my parents got home. Hopefully they wouldn't look up, or I'd be even **DEADER!**

The disco ball was rolling on the floor next to a Zombie's head. His body was upright next to him, arms crossed.

'Duuuuuude!' the Zombie head complained. 'That is not cool! My body is super unco when my head is not attached.'

'Uhhh, let me help,' I offered.

I grabbed the **ZOMBIE HEAD**, wedged it back on the body and stepped back.

Oops—I'd put it on backwards.

'Just one sec.' I leaned forwards and turned the Zombie head around. I stepped back again and said, 'Perfect!'

The Zombie just mumbled and shuffled away.

'Okay, now I gotta get this disco ball back up...' I huffed.

'Let me help,' Endaria offered. She came over with a chair and held it still while I climbed on it with the disco ball.

'DON'T BREAK THAT!' Skeletor's voice **BOOMED** through the house.

I jumped and nearly dropped it. 'No worries! I'm being super careful,' I assured him as I retaped the disco ball to another patch of ceiling.

I climbed down and then turned to Endaria, 'So... are you having a good time?'

Before she could reply, Skelee came **SPRINTING** into the living room, holding something wrapped in a towel.

'ZOMBIE! ZOMBIE! ZOMBIE!' he yelled, running straight at me. 'Zombie, you gotta come with me right now. RIGHT NOW!'

'Uh, sorry, Endaria,' I smiled, shrugged and followed Skelee to the kitchen.

'Wait here,' Skelee instructed. Skelee looked left and right. He checked the cupboards and pulled open the fridge as well.

'Okay, we're **ALONE,**' he decided.

Then he unwrapped the towel...

FRIDAY 8:38

It was a beetroot.

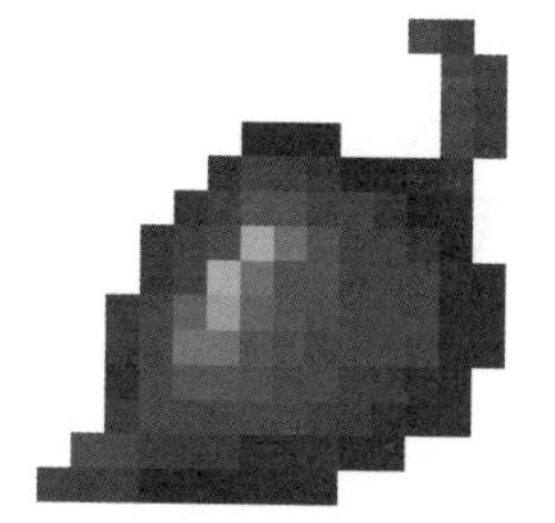

Huh? What's so great about a beetroot?

'Skelee, why did you pull me in here like *that* for *that*?' I asked, pointing at the **BEETROOT.**

'But, Zombie, look. Isn't it the most beautiful beetroot you've ever seen?'

Skelee looked hooked.

'O...kay,' I didn't really know what to say. 'Umm, Skelee, do you really want everyone out there to **EAT** your beetroot?'

'What?' Skelee looked horrified. 'No! It's mine. All mine...'

And they say I'm weird!

'Well... you stay in here with your beetroot, and I'll go give everyone else the cookies and pumpkin pie. Okay?'

I picked up the platter of cookies

and the pumpkin pie and when I turned back, Skelee was sitting on the floor, **ROCKING BACK AND FORTH,** hugging the beetroot.

'Yeah, I'm not dealing with this right now,' I mumbled to myself and walked out of the kitchen.

I set the food on the almost empty snacks table and backed away as the hungry teenage mobs pushed towards the table. Then I heard a small voice.

'SNACKS!'

I turned and saw Wesley squeezing through the crowd towards the food.

'Oh no, you don't!' I grabbed my little brother before he could bite the Skeleton blocking his way. 'You are not ruining my party. Not today! I am on a **MISSION!**' I explained to Wesley as I dragged him out of the living room, up the stairs and into his room.

I was about to shut the door when he looked up at me with his little Zombie face. His big Zombie eyes were starting to water and he looked really upset. 'I—*sniff*—just wanted—*sniff*—some snacks!' On the last word, Wesley started bawling his eyes out.

'WAAAAAAAAAAAAAAAAAAAAAAA AAAAAAAAAAAAAAAAAAAAAHH!'

I slammed the door closed, but I could still hear the wailing. I peeked down the stairs and could see mobs looking up at me.

Urgh, they could hear him. Man, is this what I sound like when I throw a **TEMPER TANTRUM?**

I opened the door again and went to Wesley, 'Shhhhh, don't worry! Zombie is here. You want food? I'll get you food.'

'Really?' he sniffled.

'Yes, of course! Just sit here—**QUIETLY**—and I will get you food!'

'Okay, Zumbie,' Wesley nodded.

I shut the door behind me, raced downstairs to the snacks table and—

ALL THE SNACKS WERE GONE!

Already?! What is wrong with these teen mobs?!

I raced back into the kitchen, stepped over Skelee and his beetroot and started rummaging through the cupboards again.

URGH! All we had left were those mushrooms! Well, desperate times...

I grabbed as many mushrooms as I could and threw them on the crafting table.

BAM!

I had four pots of mushroom stew.

I carried three pots out to the obviously starving mob kids. Then I grabbed the last pot and headed up to Wesley.

I passed Creepy on the way and said, 'Hey, uh, don't go in the kitchen. Skelee is having a **THING** with a beetroot. It's not pretty. But we can deal with it later.'

'What?' Creepy was really confused.

'Later!' I called out and headed upstairs.

True to his word, Wesley had sat there quietly playing with his Chicken while waiting. He grinned when I walked in with the pot of food. I plopped it in front of him.

'Eat, kiddo.' I sat back and watched as Wesley gobbled up the mushroom stew like he hadn't eaten in a week, instead of only two hours ago.

When he was done, I tucked him into bed and shut the door behind me. **BIG BROTHER WIN.**

Now for the party! I raced back

downstairs, but when I got back to the living room, I could barely squeeze through the doorway.

The living room was packed! It was so crowded that mobs were spilling into the front and back yards.

CRASH!

Oh no, not again! This was getting out of hand! I followed the noise, pushing to the back of the living room, and saw a massive Blaze standing in front of a shattered vase, my mum's dead flowers all over the floor. I am in **SO MUCH TROUBLE.**

'Dude, I am so sorry.' The Blaze didn't look sorry at all. 'That was totally an accident. Just, like, **BOOM!** Shattered... everywhere.' The Blaze shrugged and turned back to talk to his friend.

Urgh, now I gotta clean up this mess.

'Hey, Zombie-o, want some help-io?' Ste-Creepio popped up beside me.

'Yeah, Ste... Creepio,' I corrected myself just in time. 'That would be awesome, thanks. I just need some help cleaning this up. Wait here,

I'm gonna go get a dustpan.'

I came back a few minutes later and Ste-Creepio was gone.

URGGHHH. So much for helping!

As I was sweeping up the mess—on my **OWN,** that is—I heard a voice.

'Hey, Zombie. Whatcha doing down there?'

I looked up to see Endaria standing over me.

'Oh hey!' I jumped up and kicked

the full dustpan underneath the side table. 'Just cleaning up a bit. Don't want anyone to stand on any glass... you know...'

I cringed. **BORING!** How do I turn this conversation around?!

'Did you have any snacks?' I asked.

'No, I didn't get the chance... the food went really quickly. You must be a good chef!'

'Oh man... I *just* made cookies and pumpkin pie and mushroom stew...'

'No, it's fine. I'm sure I can rustle

something up. Actually, I'll go into the kitchen now and—'

'NO!' I cut her off. 'I don't think you should do that, I think—'

Suddenly I saw something out of the corner of my eye.

It was Ste-Creepio, lying on the ground in the corner next to Dad's **MOULD PATCH.**

Wait, was he... cleaning it?!

FRIDAY 9:20

'Ah, what is he *doing*?!' I turned to Endaria and quickly said, 'Sorry, be right back.' Then I ran in Steve's direction.

I grabbed him by his Creeper **FOOT** and dragged him into the bathroom.

'DUDE!'

'DUDE!'

'WHAT ARE YOU DOING?'

'WHAT ARE YOU DOING?'

I slammed the door behind us so we could talk without being overheard.

'Why are you **CLEANING?**'

'Why are you dragging me into bathrooms by my feet?!' Steve said from the floor.

'Fine, sorry! But more importantly, WHY ARE YOU CLEANING?!'

'You asked me to!' Steve said.

'No, I didn't!'

Steve stared at me and raised an

eyebrow. 'Yes, you did. You said, "I just need some help cleaning up".'

I thought back. Tried to use my **PEA-SIZED BRAIN.** *Think. Think. Think.*

'Oh wait, yeah I did.' I slapped my forehead. 'But I said "cleaning THIS up". I just meant the broken vase. Not all the awesome, gross stuff that's *supposed* to be here! You nearly killed my dad's mould patch. He sprays it every day and heats it up when it gets cold!'

'Oh... ew.' Steve wrinkled his nose.

'Just... stop cleaning things! Act like a mob,' I instructed.

'Okay, okay, I get it,' Steve nodded.

PHEW! Surely the worst was over now and I could go and actually enjoy my party.

BANG! CRRRRRRRRASHHHHH! CRAAACKKKKKK!

Urgh! What now?!

I yanked the door open and ran out to the living room to see the disco ball lying on the floor again and another massive chunk of the ceiling missing. Creepy was hopping by so I stopped him.

'Dude! What is in that disco ball?!'

'I dunno, man, but it must be heavy!' Creepy laughed and hopped off.

I gave up trying to retape the massive disco ball to the ceiling. Instead, I just **PLONKED** it on the empty snacks table. As I turned away, I caught sight of Wesley running into the kitchen.

'Oh no, not again!' I muttered.

I followed him into the kitchen and saw Skelee with his beetroot and Wesley with his chicken **DANCING** on the kitchen counter.

URGGHHH!

'You were supposed to be asleep,' I said to Wesley.

'But I woke up,' he explained.

'I CAN SEE THAT!' I grabbed Wesley under my arm, then turned back to Skelee. 'STAY.'

Stomping up the stairs, I plopped Wesley back in his bed and shut the door behind me. I paused for a second, thinking about locking him in with a chair against the door knob or something, but then I thought better of it. Mum would have **KILLED ME** and I was already in enough trouble.

When I went back downstairs, I went straight to the kitchen to deal with Skelee.

But Skelee was gone.

Oh boy.

I popped out of the kitchen and saw Creepy talking to some of our classmates in the hallway. I ran over and dragged him away, into the kitchen, 'Later is now, Creepy. **LATER IS NOW!'**

'Dude, what are you talking about?'

'When I was making snacks before, Skelee offered to go harvest a beetroot. When he came back he was really obsessed with the beetroot he'd gotten. He couldn't think of anything else.'

'Hmm, sounds familiar,' Creepy said.

I looked at him blankly. Huh?

'Anyway,' I continued, 'it must have been **MAGIC** or something cause now he's gone!'

'What do you mean, "he's gone"? Where did he go?'

'I don't know, man! He was rocking back and forth, holding the beetroot like it was the only thing in the Overworld that mattered to him.'

WREEEEP, WROOOOP!

What was that?! I poked my head into the hallway and saw a blue and red light flashing outside the open front door.

Uh oh. This was not good.

'What's happening?' Creepy asked. He followed me out to the front yard, where there was a big car with a flashing blue and red light on top.

Getting out of the car was a **POLICE OFFICER.**

FRIDAY 9:42

'The name is Officer Ricky D. Bones. I'm just here to check up on some **NOISE COMPLAINTS,**' the Skeleton explained.

Busted!

'What? I didn't complain about the noise!' I said.

'No, not you,' Officer Bones said. 'One of your neighbours.' He paused. 'Why would you complain about your **OWN PARTY?** That makes no sense. Anyway, I'm going to have to take a look inside.'

'Sure...' As the officer walked past, I looked at Creepy and mouthed, *'What do we do?'*

'What?'

I mouthed it slower. *'What. Do. We. Do?'*

'Dude, I can't hear you. The music is **TOO LOUD.**'

'Creepy! What do we do?!' I yelled.

'Dude, it's fine. We haven't done anything wrong except make a little noise. Let him look around, no problem!' Creepy shrugged.

He was so calm! He must have taken his Liquid Nitrogen Inhaler before he came. I was still nervous, but I didn't say anything as we followed the officer into the house.

He stopped in the living room.

I cringed, waiting for the

CRACK DOWN.

'Wait a second... turn that song up,' he gestured at the Wither kid standing near the stereo.

The latest hit song from *Braaaaaains* blared from the speakers.

Huh?

'I LOVE THIS SONG!' Suddenly the bass dropped in the song, and so did Officer Ricky D. Bones. He started hitting the floor... hard. I could hear his bones

CLACKING as he danced.
'WOOO! TURN IT UP, KIDS!
WOOOOO!'

'Uhhh, I vote we put this song on repeat and leave Officer Bones to it,' I said.

'Yep,' Creepy agreed.

I snuck over to the stereo and punched the repeat button a bunch of times. Then I snuck back to Creepy.

'Now... we need to find Skelee,' I said. 'Let's get Slimey and Steve so they can help.'

'Wait, Steve's here?' Creepy asked.

'Yeah,' I said. 'Keep an eye out for a **FUNNY LOOKING CREEPER** who ends everything with "io".'

Creepy didn't look impressed.

Ten minutes later, we met back in the same spot, with Slimey and Steve in tow.

Creepy eyed Steve's costume and wrinkled his nose, 'That's, like, borderline offensive.'

'Really?' Steve asked, looking down at his costume. 'I tried so hard to make it look real. I guess I need to study Creepers more.'

'Okay, guys. The new mission is to find Skelee. He's holding a small beetroot. Last I saw, he was sitting on the kitchen floor, rocking back and forth, **HUGGING** it. He can't have gone far,' I said in my drill sergeant voice.

We agreed to meet back in the same spot in ten minutes. Then we split up.

I was wandering through the house when I had an idea. The only time Skelee had stopped rocking was when **WESLEY** went into the kitchen.

I ran upstairs to Wesley's room and opened the door to find Wesley and Skelee playing with Wesley's Chicken and Skelee's beetroot.

'Skelee! I found you!' I said happily. 'You need to come with me!'

'No,' Skelee shook his head. 'Me and my beetroot are staying here. We're having fun.'

'What? Skelee, snap out of it!' I grabbed his arm and tried to drag him out of the room, but the bony guy was a lot stronger than he looked. He stayed put.

Suddenly I had an idea. I reached forwards and **SNATCHED** the beetroot out of his hands.

'You want the beetroot? Fine, come and get the beetroot!' I dashed out of Wesley's room and down the stairs. I heard a clacking noise, which meant that Skelee was following me. I ran along the hallway to the meeting point.

'Guys, I found Skelee! I—'

THUD!

Skelee tackled me to the ground.

'GIVE ME BACK MY BEETROOT!' Skelee scrabbled at the floor, reaching for the beetroot that had fallen out of my hand when I hit the ground.

'Dude! You can't do stuff like that, one of my limbs could fall off!' I said, standing up and dusting myself off.

'Sorry,' Skelee said, stroking his

beetroot. 'I just love it so much.'

I looked at the guys, mouthing '*See?*'

The guys all shrugged.

There was a pause in the music as the song clicked back to the beginning, and in the quiet we could suddenly hear **CHANTING AND STOMPING.** We looked at each other, then I led the way out the front door towards the noise.

There were funny looking Villagers in the front yard. I looked at

Steve. 'What are they? They don't look like normal Villagers.'

Steve turned pale. 'They're not. They're **PILLAGERS!**'

We're doomed!

'What—' I started to say, but I was cut off as one of them started yelling.

'THEY MAY TAKE OUR DROPS, BUT THEY'LL NEVER... TAKE... OUR FREEEEEDOM!! ATTACK!!'

And suddenly the Pillagers were **CHARGING** at my front door.

'AHHHHHHHHH!'

We ran back inside and slammed the door shut behind us.

'What are those things?!' Creepy hissed.

'Pillagers are Illagers, but with **CROSSBOWS,**' said Steve. 'At least they won't open the door. They never do in raids.'

'Okay, you guys stay here!' I made

Slimey, Skelee, Creepy and Steve hold the front door shut against the Pillagers and ran into the living room.

'OFFICER BONES! WE NEED HELP!' I screamed.

He couldn't hear me. He was breaking it down on the dancefloor. I could even see little drops of **SWEAT** on his skull.

I didn't know Skeletons could sweat...

I ran over to the stereo and pulled the plug out of the wall, stopping the music.

'Dude, that was dramatic,' a Blaze pointed out. 'There's a pause button right there.'

'Alright, fine, thanks for your help,' I snapped at her. Then I turned to Officer Bones. 'Officer! We need help, it's **URGENT!**'

'That was my jam! I was breaking it down!' Officer Bones whined.

'Sometimes, I just need a break from work, okay? Everytime something bad happens, it's always "Officer Bones this" and "Officer Bones that"!'

'THERE'S A STAMPEDE OF PILLAGERS OUTSIDE!'

'What?' Officer Bones stood up straight. 'Why didn't you say that first?!'

He ran towards the hallway and stopped when he saw the guys holding the front door shut.

'SITREP!' he barked.

'What?' Steve asked.

'I dunno,' Slimey shrugged.

Creepy was hyperventilating now. Man, I hope he brought his Inhaler with him. We have enough problems without a Creeper **EXPLOSION** too!

'SITREP! It means situation report! Tell me what's going on!' Officer Bones commanded.

We all started talking at once.

'There are a ton of Pillagers and—'

'I think one of them was wearing a top hat—'

'He started screaming about drops and freedom—'

'They're invading—'

'STOP!' Officer Bones boomed. 'I was in there, having myself a great old **BOOGIE,** and you mob kids ruined it for me. The least you can do is tell me one at a time. You first.' He pointed straight at me.

'Well, first there was Skelee and his beetroot. He went and harvested the beetroot, then came back to the party and got really—'

'CUT TO THE CHASE!'

'I don't know anything! We were outside and saw a bunch of Pillagers charging at us. So we ran inside and got you!' I said quickly.

'Okay, this is doable,' Officer Bones mumbled.

'Sure,' I said.

Then I realised he was talking to himself. Was Officer Bones giving himself... a **PEP TALK?!**

'You can do this. You're a police officer. Officer Bones. The Officer Bones.'

I leaned around to look at Steve, who just raised his **EYEBROW** at me and shrugged.

'Uh, Officer Bones?' I asked.

'Just give me a minute,' he snapped.

I looked at Steve again. He didn't seem to know what to do either.

I peeked out the window. All the

Pillagers were standing around chatting to each other, leaning on their weapons.

'Why are they even here?' Slimey asked. 'Why would they come to a mob party?'

'Well, duh. Why do you think? A ton of different mobs all in the one place? Imagine the **DROPS!**' Steve shrugged.

Officer Bones stopped mumbling and stared at Steve.

'Umm, I mean... the drops-io,' Steve gulped.

'Ste-Creepio,' I said, trying to keep Steve's identity hidden. 'Do you know how the Pillagers might have found out that a lot of different mobs would be in the one house today?'

'Oh man, uh, that's a big guess for me to, uh, make...io,' Steve stuttered.

'STE-CREEPIO!' I snapped.

'Okay, fine. Say, for example, a certain **HUMAN** was invited to the mob party. Perhaps that Human might have mentioned it to his friend Alex at Human School, and his Human teacher, Master Sergeant

Fuller B. Loney, *could* have overheard and *could* have, maybe, possibly, perhaps, **RALLIED** the Pillagers.'

I gasped. 'Not the crazy guy that teaches "How to Annihilate Mobs and Eradicate Them from Existence"?! Please tell me you didn't tell Alex during his class!'

We are in serious trouble

Steve shrugged, looking sheepish.

URGH! I put my head in my hands.

'And now we have a bunch of Pillagers outside the house wanting to kill us for our drops. Great,' Creepy dead-panned.

'I know. I have an idea!' Skelee stood up. He took a deep breath (I don't know why since he doesn't need to breathe), gripped his beetroot tight and then yanked the front door open. He pulled back his arm and hurled the beetroot through the air.

It landed with a bounce in front of a Pillager and...

NOTHING HAPPENED.

Everyone stared at it.

'Oh.' Skelee looked disappointed. 'That really did nothing.'

We pulled Skelee back inside and slammed the door shut.

'Why did you do that?' I asked.

'I dunno. I felt like the beetroot was magical, so maybe it could wipe them all out for us.'

Then Skelee pulled the nearby window open and leaned out. 'If, by any chance, you aren't using that **AVERAGE** beetroot I just threw at you, could you please throw it back? It would be very much appreciated, thanks!'

Skelee waited a moment before pulling his head back in. 'I'm gonna let them think about it.'

'I have an idea,' Officer Bones finally said. 'We build a moat.'

'A moat?' I asked.

'A moat,' Officer Bones confirmed.

'A moat...'

'Basically, we dig a really deep trench around the house, and then bait the Pillagers to fall into it. They won't survive the **FALL DAMAGE,'** Officer Bones explained.

'Oh. That's surprisingly simple,' I said. 'Alright, guys, let's do this. Creepy, Slimey, Steve, you guys stick together. Skelee and Officer Bones, you're with me.'

'Who's Steve?' Officer Bones tried

to frown... which was impossible because he was a Skeleton and didn't have eyebrows.

'Uhhh, I mean Ste-Creepio! Sorry, I was thinking of Pillagers and Humans and said the wrong thing. Hahaha,' I said, trying to throw Officer Bones off.

Steve looked like he wanted to punch me.

'Alright, team. We can do this! **LET'S SAVE THE OVERWORLD!** Well, everyone in this house anyway.'

'Or die trying!' Skelee cried.

'Uhh, I'm not so keen on that,' I said.

'Come on, **FACE FACTS**, Zombie.' Skelee shrugged and headed to the back door.

FRIDAY 10:14

We'd agreed my team would dig to the left, Creepy's team would dig to the right and we'd meet in the middle and then somehow get all the Pillagers to fall into the **MOAT.** Luckily, they were only in front of the house, so we could sneak out the back door.

My team had been digging for fifteen minutes and only made about a metre's progress when

Steve broke through the dirt in front of us.

Huh? He's better at this **MINING THING** than I thought. He'd circled the house by himself!

'Come on. I left the others in the front...io,' Steve said.

When we reached them, I explained the plan. 'Okay, on the count of three, we climb out and run to the front door. The Pillagers will see us, chase us and then fall into the pit.'

I started the count: '1... 2... 3!'

We all scrabbled over the edge of the trench and **BOLTED** into the house. When we were almost at the front door, I realised that none of the Pillagers were chasing us. They were just watching. They could have been at a show! Except for the axes and other weapons, that is.

What was going on?

I stopped running and grabbed Skelee. 'We need to get them to chase us so they fall into the trench!' I shout-whispered.

'You go inside with the others. I have a plan.' Skelee took another deep (but useless) breath. Then he ran straight at the Pillagers. He **LEAPT** over the trench in one jump, his bony arms raised in the air like wings.

We all rushed through the door, but left it open a crack to watch what happened.

Skelee bounded around the Pillagers, **DODGING** their attacks. Finally, he stopped, bent down, then stood and bolted back towards us. The Pillagers roared and gave chase.

As he leapt over the trench again, I could see what was curled into his bony little fist.

His beetroot.

I couldn't believe it. But it worked— they were chasing him!

'YEAH, SKELEE! WOO! GET THAT BEETROOT!' I cheered.

The other guys started cheering and whooping too, as Skelee flew through the front door unharmed.

We continued to stand near the door and watched as, one-by-one, the Pillagers ran head first into the trench and **DISAPPEARED.**

In seconds, my front yard was Pillager free. Sergeant Fuller B. Loney had disappeared too.

'WOO, YEAH, WE DID IT! WOO!'

We all cheered and high-fived, including Officer Bones.

He used the walkie-talkie on his shoulder to report back to the police station. 'Officer Bones here. Just letting you know there was a Pillager attack and I survived and it was **WICKED!**'

'Roger that, Officer Bones. Could you give us more information? Do you need back-up? Repeat, do you need back-up?' the radio crackled.

But Officer Bones turned off the walkie-talkie and did a little

VICTORY DANCE. 'We did it! You guys are awesome. You should all be police officers when you grow up. I can't wait to tell my mates about this!'

Then Officer Bones headed out the door. As he left, he found a plank of wood and dumped it across the trench so he could get to his car.

We all waved him goodbye. And as we did, we noticed...

Oh no.

My mum and dad were back.

FRIDAY 10:51

'What is going on?!' my mum yelled as she saw the police officer getting into his car and the giant trench around the house.

I turned and dashed into the living room. 'EVERYONE NEEDS TO LEAVE! NOW! MY MUM AND DAD ARE HERE! GO! GO! GO!'

I never dreamed that the house could have emptied so quickly, but the threat of **PARENTS** cleared everyone out. I saw Skeletor scoop up the disco ball on his way out.

It was only when everyone was out the back door that I saw the **DISASTER** left behind.

And so did my mum and dad as they walked in behind me. Endaria's mum followed, confused.

The living room had chunks of the ceiling missing and blocks scattered all over the floor. Mum's dead flowers were squashed and the dustpan holding pieces of the smashed vase was half sticking out from under the side table.

Dad's mould patch was almost gone, the white wall standing out against the normal **GRIME.** For some reason, Wesley was sitting in a pot of mushroom stew, covered in it from head to toe.

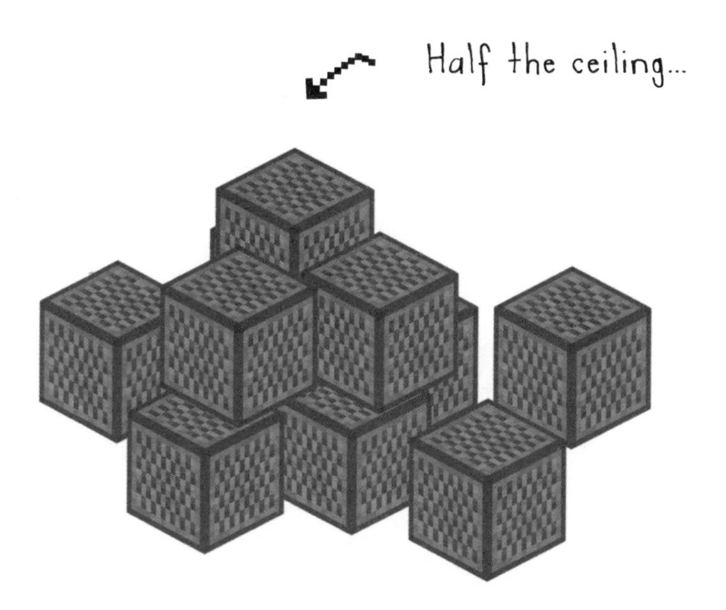

'Zackary Julius Zombie...' my mum growled through gritted teeth. Man, I didn't even realise she still had teeth!

I knew it then. I was going to be **GROUNDED** until I was Old Man Jenkins' age.

At least Endaria had disappeared somewhere so she wouldn't see my shame.

SATURDAY

Turned out I was only grounded for a month.

But I did have to fix everything up. Lucky Steve is as good at **BUILDING** as he is at mining! He was inside fixing the ceiling; I was outside filling in the trench.

While I was shovelling, Endaria came to sit outside with me.

'Hey.'

'Hey,' I replied.

'So, you're in a lot of trouble, huh?'

'Yeah,' I nodded. 'But it's not too bad. This is pretty standard.'

'Oh. Then I guess the party was worth it, huh?'

'Well, I didn't get to do everything I wanted,' I shrugged. If I had a heart, I think it would have been **BEATING** really fast.

'Oh? What else would you have done?' Endaria asked.

'Spent more time hanging out with you.' I gulped and went for it. 'That's the whole reason I threw this party... for you.'

'Oh.' She thought about it for a moment.

I went back to shovelling.
The **SUSPENSE!**

'Thanks for throwing the party,' Endaria finally said. 'But I wish I could have spent more time talking to you too. Actually, I tried to talk to you all night. But you kept saying "be right back" and running off.'

'But I was just trying to make it the best party ever so you'd think I was cool!' I wailed.

Endaria shrugged. 'Well, I mean, I had fun, but it would have been more fun if you'd just relaxed so we could hang out and chat.'

Wait, isn't that what Steve told me to do? Just talk to her? **BE MYSELF?**

I really need to listen to Steve more often.

'Anyway, it's not the end of the world,' Endaria went on. 'Mum says she likes this area and we might stay here. Get our own place. Go to Scare School and everything. So we'll have plenty of chances to hang out, if you want to.'

I almost choked. She must like me! I did it! **MISSION ACCOMPLISHED!**

I jumped up and did a victory fist pump.

'Uhh, Zombie?' Endaria asked.

Oh... right.

'Yes, I'd love to hang out!'

I could see it all now.

Next time...

Endaria smiled. As she turned to go back inside, she said, 'Oh, by the way, Skelee is still in Wesley's room with his beetroot. You should probably go talk to him...'

URRGGGHHHH!

DIARY OF A MINECRAFT ZOMBIE

Take a peek into the diary of Zack Zombie. He's just like any other kid, except he's a lot more **DEAD**!

COLLECT THEM ALL!

☑ GOT IT!

☑ GOT IT!

☑ GOT IT!

☑ GOT IT!

☑ GOT IT!

☑ GOT IT!

☑ GOT IT!

☑ GOT IT!

☑ GOT IT!

☑ GOT IT!

☑ GOT IT! ☑ GOT IT! ☑ GOT IT! ☑ GOT IT! ☑ GOT IT!

☑ GOT IT! ☑ GOT IT! ☑ GOT IT! ☑ GOT IT! ☑ GOT IT!

☑ GOT IT! ☑ GOT IT! ☑ GOT IT! ☑ GOT IT! ☑ GOT IT!

☑ GOT IT! ☑ GOT IT! ☑ GOT IT! ☐ GOT IT! ☐ GOT IT!

FIND OUT WHAT HAPPENS NEXT!

Boogieman's Big Top circus is in town! Zombie can't wait to get involved.

BUT WHEN ZOMBIE'S MUM DISAPPEARS, CAN ZOMBIE HOLD IT ALL TOGETHER, FIND HIS MUM AND PULL OFF THE CRAZIEST ACT IN THE CIRCUS?